DRAGONBORN
Monster Hunter

BY MICHAEL DAHL
ILLUSTRATED BY LUIGI AIME

RAINTREE IS AN IMPRINT OF CAPSTONE GLOBAL LIBRARY LIMITED, A COMPANY INCORPORATED IN
ENGLAND AND WALES HAVING ITS REGISTERED OFFICE AT 264 BANBURY ROAD, OXFORD, OX2 7DY -
REGISTERED COMPANY NUMBER: 6695582

WWW.RAINTREE.CO.UK
MYORDERS@RAINTREE.CO.UK

TEXT © CAPSTONE GLOBAL LIBRARY LIMITED 2019
THE MORAL RIGHTS OF THE PROPRIETOR HAVE BEEN ASSERTED.

ART DIRECTOR: KAY FRASER
GRAPHIC DESIGNER: HILARY WACHOLZ
PRODUCTION SPECIALIST: KATHY MCCOLLEY
ORIGINAL ILLUSTRATIONS © 2013
ILLUSTRATED BY LUIGI AIME
ORIGINATED BY CAPSTONE GLOBAL LIBRARY LTD
Printed and bound in the United Kingdom.

ISBN 978 1 4747 7148 1
22 21 20 19 18
10 9 8 7 6 5 4 3 2 1

BRITISH LIBRARY CATALOGUING IN PUBLICATION DATA
A FULL CATALOGUE RECORD FOR THIS BOOK IS AVAILABLE FROM THE BRITISH LIBRARY.

ACKNOWLEDGEMENTS
SHUTTERSTOCK: CAESART (METAL PLATE, PP. 1, 4, 66); FERNANDO CORTES (DRAGON PATTERN)

CONTENTS

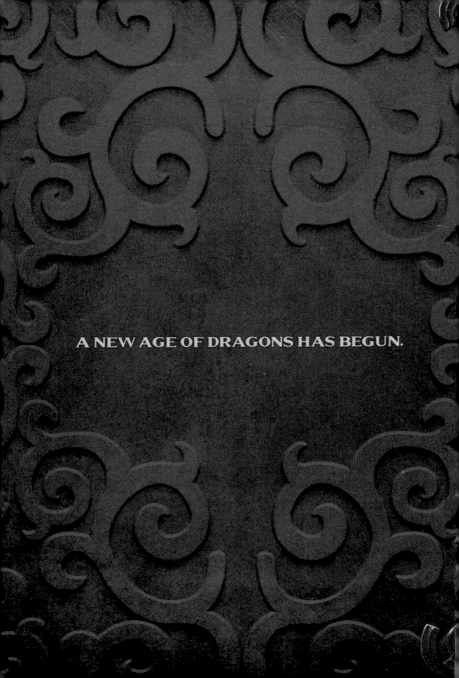

A NEW AGE OF DRAGONS HAS BEGUN.

DRAGONBORN

Young people around the world
have discovered that dragon blood
flows in their veins. They are filled
with new power and new ideas.
But before they reveal themselves
to the world, they must find one
another . . .

CHAPTER 1
Many warnings

Ren heard the warning from a TV screen.

He was watching the news while he was on the train.

The superfast train was taking him from school into the city.

"Real monsters," said the news announcer.

"Creatures that look like you or me, but can change in the blink of an eye."

Ren looked around the train carriage. He was surrounded by a crowd of people.

Were they staring at him?

"These creatures may look like
humans. But they are not," the
announcer went on. "I know it
sounds unbelievable, but doctors have
discovered a strange new blood disease.
A disease that comes from lizards."

A man standing next to Ren nodded his head. He was also watching the TV.

The man turned to his friends. They were young businessmen in suits, carrying briefcases.

"It's about the monsters," the man said.

"They're dangerous," said one of the other businessmen.

"They killed an old woman in my neighbourhood," said another. "I heard it on the news."

"And I heard they eat small children," added a third.

Ren felt hot.

The men's talk was making him angry.

But he had to be careful. He had to control his emotions.

Ren knew that whenever strong feelings flooded through him, he started to change.

The train suddenly slowed down.

Ren bumped into one of the businessmen.

The man frowned and looked down at Ren.

"Sorry," said Ren.

The TV news presenter continued. "The creatures are easy to identify. Each one has a strange birthmark on its body."

Ren realized he was rubbing his arm.

It was the arm with the birthmark.

Did the men on the train know what
he was hiding?

The businessman was still staring
down at Ren.

He had an odd look on his face.

"What's wrong with your eyes?" asked the man.

Ren stared back at the man.

In the man's glasses, Ren could see a reflection of his own eyes.

They were turning yellow.

They looked like lizard's eyes.

The train stopped.

Quickly, Ren jumped off.

He looked back as the train doors hissed shut.

He saw the businessmen through the windows. They were still talking.

Then one of them turned and pointed at Ren.

They knew.

CHAPTER 2
Secret companions

"Hey, you!" someone shouted.

Ren turned and froze.

He saw a dragon.

A giant poster covered one wall of the train station.

The poster displayed an evil-looking
dragon.

It had red wings and was spitting fire.

Words on the poster read:

THEY ARE EVERYWHERE

THEY ARE EVERYWHERE

モンスター

More words read:

IF YOU SUSPECT ANYONE OF BEING A

DANGER, CALL THE POLICE

"You! Hey!" came a shout.

A teenage boy, the same age as Ren, ran up to him.

"Are you Ren?" the boy asked. Then, with a shy smile, he added, "I'm Kazu."

Ren nodded nervously. "I think someone on the train knew me," he said. "I mean, they knew what I was."

Kazu looked at Ren's jacket.

"But your arms are covered," Kazu said. "No one would see. Let's go and get something to eat."

The two boys hurried along towards a huge shopping centre.

"The food hall is over there," said Kazu.

"I need to stop at the cash machine," said Ren.

"Look," said Kazu. "There they are."

Ren saw two strangers walking towards them, a boy and a girl.

"I'm Hiro," said the boy. "And this is Aya," he added, pointing at the girl.

"I can speak for myself," said Aya.

She smiled at Ren, and he smiled back.

"Is this the first time any of us have met each other?" Aya asked.

They all nodded.

Ren had chatted online with each of them. They had found one another through a special website.

This was the first day they had met in person. They had to.

It was getting dangerous to be them. They had to stick together.

"My school was having a special inspection," Ren said, walking next to Aya. "The nurse was going to look at every pupil, and check for birthmarks."

"My school, too," said Hiro.

He looked at the others. "I don't know what I'll tell my parents. How can I go back home now?"

Aya stopped walking. "I hate that!" she snapped.

A dragon poster hung above their heads. "That's so unfair," she said.

"Quiet," said Kazu. "You'll get us into trouble."

"Where's Yoko?" Ren asked.

"Don't worry," said Kazu. "She is meeting us there."

A horrible scream ripped through the air.

Then the young people heard someone shout: "The monster! The monster!"

The scream came from the food hall.

CHAPTER 3
The hunters

"Yoko!" shouted Aya.

Ren and the others rushed down some stairs.

They could see a girl. She stood in the centre of the food hall.

A mob of people surrounded her in a wide circle.

A young boy was crying, pointing at her. "She has monster eyes!" he wailed.

"No! No, I don't!" said the girl.

Two police officers walked up to the girl.

Ren watched them grab her arms.

"That is Yoko," said Aya. "She told us she'd be carrying a yellow bag."

"Not so loud," said Kazu. "We can't let people know we know her."

"We have to help her," said Aya.

But how? wondered Ren.

"If we try to help her, then the hunters will grab us too," said Hiro.

Ren felt the birthmark on his arm begin to burn.

If he transformed here, and people saw what he was, then what would happen? He thought about the dragon posters. *Danger.*

"Oh no!" said Hiro.

The two police officers stepped back quickly from Yoko.

She seems taller, thought Ren.

She *was* taller.

Taller and taller the girl grew.

Two huge wings unfolded from her shoulders.

Someone in the crowd screamed.

Someone else threw a food tray.

The crowd scattered in fear as the girl dragon rose into the air.

The dragon's wings flapped loudly.

The rush of air knocked over chairs and tables. Potted plants rolled on the floor.

Ren looked up.

There was no way for the dragon to escape. The ceiling was covered with thick glass and metal tubes.

"She can't get out," Ren said to Hiro.

The dragon screamed.

She lowered her scaly jaws and opened her mouth wide.

A stream of fire shot towards the floor.

Before Ren could move, three men pushed past him.

They wore uniforms with dark helmets.

Each of them held a strange weapon.

As the men ran, they surrounded the rising dragon.

"Look!" shouted a young woman. "It's the monster hunters!"

One of the men made a sharp gesture with his hand.

Then all three of them raised their weapons.

The dragon roared.

The weapons fired.

Dark metal nets shot out at the creature.

The dragon tried to fly away, but it was too late.

The nets had done their work. They weighed down the creature's wings.

"That's what could happen to us," Hiro said softly.

The creature sank back to the floor of the food hall.

More men in uniforms ran out of the shadows.

"We have to get out of here," whispered Kazu.

"This way," said Aya.

CHAPTER 4
Hiding

A few moments later, the four teenagers were outside the shopping centre.

Lightning flashed in the sky.

They hid in an alleyway.

They crouched down behind rubbish bins.

"Now what do we do?" asked Hiro.

"We can't go home."

"Why not?" asked Kazu.

Hiro pulled off his jacket. "Because of this," he said.

He showed his bare arm to the others. They looked at his dragon-shaped birthmark.

Ren pulled off his jacket and revealed his own mark.

Then Kazu did, and then Aya.

"We're all the same," said Ren. "The same as Yoko. That's why we have to stick together."

Lightning flashed again in the sky.

Hiro grinned. "Maybe we should all change," he said. "And fly out of here."

Aya shook her head. "Someone would see us," she said.

"I can fly fast," Hiro said.

"Those net guns were pretty fast, too," said Aya.

"I'm not very good at flying," said Kazu. He stared up at the sky.

"I could help you," Ren said. "We all could."

Aya stood up. "No, she said. "We have to find a place to hide."

A siren sounded nearby.

Ren stood up next to Aya. "I think we better go now," he said.

CHAPTER 5
On the run

The sirens got louder.

"It's the hunters," said Ren.

They ran down the alley. "Now where?" said Hiro.

Aya led them down another alley.

The sky grew dark above them.

Streetlights blinked on along the streets. The group saw dark vans speeding through the streets.

When the vans stopped, crews of men jumped out.

The men wore uniforms and carried weapons.

The four dragonteens stayed in the shadows.

When they reached busy streets, they tried to blend in with the walking crowds.

They didn't want anyone to notice them.

They came to a big, busy junction. Vans were parked everywhere.

Bright streetlights and neon signs lit up the night.

"I don't like it here," whispered Hiro. "Where exactly are we going?"

"Here!" shouted Aya. She shouted again. "Here! Over here!" She waved her arms above her head.

It's a trap! thought Ren. "What are you doing?" he cried.

Aya turned and looked at the others. "Freaks!" she said. "You're monsters. You're not human."

"But you're one of us," said Ren.

"I *was* one of you," said Aya. "But then I was cured. The doctors helped me. And that's what they'll do with you, if they decide not to destroy you."

The hunters were coming closer.

"No!" shouted Hiro.

He raised his arms in the air and groaned. His body thickened and grew larger. Dark wings sprang out from his shoulders.

The monster hunters ran towards him and raised their weapons.

Kazu gripped Ren's shoulder. "We have to go!" he said.

Hiro had disappeared, and the dragon stood in his place. The creature lifted its mighty head. Flames shot from between rows of fangs.

A van caught on fire. A group of hunters surrounded the monster.

"Now!" shouted their leader.

Metal nets wrapped tightly around the dragon's huge body.

The creature span around and
around. It tried to escape the netting.

Its sharp wings tore through some of
the metal strands. "Look out!" yelled one
of the hunters.

More hunters appeared. They shot net
after net at the creature.

The dragon roared in frustration.

CHAPTER 6
Falling rain

Aya turned and pointed.

"There's two more!" she yelled. "Don't let them get away."

The two boys ran.

Rain poured down on the city streets.

Kazu ran like a deer, and Ren followed close behind.

They soon reached a park in the middle of the city. They rushed into the bushes.

Ren's lungs felt like fire. "Wait, wait," he said, panting. "Maybe we should do what Hiro said. Maybe we should fly out of here."

Kazu looked up at the dark sky. Rain poured onto his face.

"Don't be scared," said Ren. "I'll help."

"But –" said Kazu.

Then Ren saw it. Rain flowed down Kazu's arm.

His dragon birthmark was washing away.

Another trap!

"You!" cried Ren.

Kazu shook his head. "No. I'm not like Aya," he said. "I've always liked dragons. They're noble. They're powerful. My brother is one, and I always wanted to be like him. But I'm not."

"I don't understand," said Ren.

"I went on the website to help," Kazu said. "To help people like my brother." He smiled. "You can come home with me," he said. "My family knows about my brother, and they don't care. You'll find a safe place there."

Ren thought hard.

There was nowhere else to go.

Moments later, flashes of lightning revealed a dragon rising from the city park.

And from the monster's claws hung a wide-eyed teenage boy.

AUTHOR

Michael Dahl is the author of more than 200 books for children and young adults. He has won the AEP Distinguished Achievement Award three times for his non-fiction. His Finnegan Zwake mystery series was shortlisted twice by the Anthony and Agatha awards. He has also written the Dragonblood series. He is a featured speaker at conferences around the United States on graphic novels and high-interest books for boys.

ILLUSTRATOR

Luigi Aime was born in 1987 in Savigliano, a small Italian city near Turin. Even at the age of three, he loved to draw. He attended art school, graduating with honours in Illustration and Animation from the European Institute of Design in Milan, Italy.

DISCUSSION QUESTIONS

1. Why did Aya, Ren, Kazu and Hiro meet?

2. Why were people with dragon blood being hunted?

3. What questions do you still have about this story? Discuss them!

WRITING PROMPTS

1. What happens after this book ends? Write a short story that extends the story.

2. It can be very interesting to think about a story from another person's point of view. Try writing this story, or part of it, from Aya's point of view. What does she see, hear, think and say? What does she notice? How is the story different?

3. Create a cover for a book. It can be this book or another book you like, or a made-up book. Write the information on the back, and include the author and illustrator names.

GLOSSARY

birthmark mark on the skin that has been there since birth

gesture action that communicates an idea or feeling

identify recognize or tell what something is or who someone is

mob large group of people

noble impressive or magnificent in appearance

reflection image seen in a shiny surface such as a mirror

revealed showed or brought into view

surrounded grouped around something

unbelievable hard to accept as true

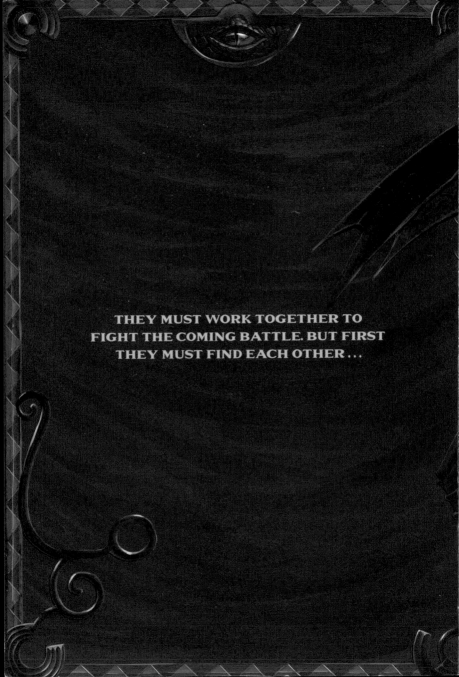

THEY MUST WORK TOGETHER TO
FIGHT THE COMING BATTLE. BUT FIRST
THEY MUST FIND EACH OTHER ...

REN YAMAMOTO

Ren was bullied by a group of boys one afternoon after school. When he got home, he washed his face in the pond in his family's garden. His reflection was not human. Since then, he has been more afraid of himself than of anyone – or anything – else.

Age: 16
Hometown: Tokyo, Japan
Dragon appearance: Blue and black
Dragon species: *Draconis potentia* ("power dragon")
Strength: Super-powerful wings

DRAGONBLOOD
RUNS THROUGH THEIR VEINS...